From the movie

Disney FROZEN

OLAF'S PERFECT SUMMER DAY

PaRragon

Bath · New York · Cologne · Melbourne · Delhi
Hong Kong · Shenzhen · Singapore · Amsterdam

This edition published by Parragon Books Ltd in 2015

Parragon Books Ltd
Chartist House
15–17 Trim Street
Bath BA1 1HA, UK
www.parragon.com

ISBN 978-1-4748-1092-0

Printed in China

Olaf's Perfect Summer Day

Summer had finally arrived in Arendelle. Everyone in the kingdom was enjoying the long sunny days after a very cold winter season. But today was going to be the hottest day of the year so far! Most of the villagers wanted to stay inside where it was cool....

But Olaf could hardly wait to get outside!
This was the kind of day he had always
dreamed of!

Olaf ran into Princess Anna's room, calling out with excitement.
"Anna, Anna! Guess what today is? It's the perfect summery day!
Let's go outside and play!"

Anna groaned as she sat up in bed. "It's so hot and sticky, Olaf."
But she had to smile when she saw Olaf's hopeful face.

Together, Olaf and Anna went to look for Queen Elsa.
They found her in the Great Hall.

"There you are, Elsa!" Olaf cried out, joyfully.

Olaf looked up shyly at the dignitary standing with Elsa.
"Hi, my name is Olaf and I like warm hugs."

"H-h-hello," the dignitary stammered in surprise.
He had never seen a talking snowman before.

Olaf turned back to Elsa. "And today is the best day for warm hugs because it's sunny and hot. Please can we go play in the sunshine?"

Elsa laughed. "That sounds like fun, Olaf. What did you have in mind?"

"It's so hot outside, though. Couldn't you cool things down just a bit, Elsa?" Anna looked hopefully at her sister.

"But Olaf's always wanted to experience heat. Shouldn't we give him his special day?" Elsa reasoned. "We'll do everything he's always wanted to do in summer!"

"Yeah, you're right," agreed Anna. "How about a picnic on the shores of the fjord?"

Olaf clasped his hands with glee. "Oooo, I love picnics!"

Anna, Elsa and Olaf trooped to the royal kitchens for picnic supplies.
They found Gerda with her head in the icebox.

"Gerda, what on Earth are you doing?" asked Elsa.

Gerda popped her head up. "Trying to keep myself cool. It's so terribly hot!"

Olaf giggled. "Did you bake cookies today?"

Gerda shook her head. "Oh, it's too hot for baking."

Elsa glanced at Olaf. She didn't want to disappoint him. "How about an ice-cold lemonade instead?" she suggested.

Olaf was thrilled. "Oooo, I love lemonade!"

Olaf, Anna and Elsa set off for their picnic adventure. At the royal gardens, a few children were lying on the field, too hot to play games.

But Olaf didn't notice. Giggling delightedly, he ran to them. "Hi, my name is Olaf. Don't you just love summer?" The children were charmed by Olaf, chasing butterflies and blowing fuzz off dandelions.

Even Elsa and Anna couldn't resist joining in.

After a while, Anna plopped down on the grass. "Whew! I'm ready for our picnic!"

Elsa agreed. "Yes, let's head to the docks. We can sail to the fjord."

Olaf, who had been chasing a bumblebee, stopped in his tracks. "We're going sailing? I've always wanted to try sailing!"

At the docks, Anna and Elsa chose a beautiful sailboat. As they set sail, Olaf hummed happily. He even got to steer the boat!

When they reached the shore, Anna set up the picnic. But Olaf couldn't sit still. "Don't you just love the feeling of sand on your snow, Anna?" he squealed. "Let's make sand angels together!"

Anna gingerly stuck a toe in the sand. "Oh, goodness, that is … uh … warm!" she squeaked. She danced on tiptoe over to the fjord's edge. "Ah, this is better," she said, as water washed over her feet.

The three friends spent the whole afternoon playing in the summer sun.

They built sandcastles and sand people.

They chased waves on the shore.

They even danced with seagulls.

And finally, when they'd tired themselves out, Anna, Elsa and Olaf had a picnic on the shores of the fjord. "Hands down, this is the best day of my life," said Olaf.

As they sailed back to Arendelle, the setting sun made
beautiful colours in the sky. Olaf was amazed. "I wish I could
hug the summer sun. I bet it would feel wonderful!"

Anna smiled as she pushed her sweaty hair off her face.
"You might need a bigger snow flurry for that, Olaf."

Back at the docks, Kristoff and Sven were waiting. They had spent the afternoon harvesting mountain lakes. Now their sledge was full of ice. Jumping out of the boat, Anna flung herself down on the delicious cold blocks. "Oh, I am glad to see you!"

Olaf told Kristoff and Sven all about their adventures and then sighed with happiness. "I wish it could always be summer!" he said.

"Summer is wonderful," Elsa agreed, smiling at Anna's antics. "But tomorrow, I predict a chance of snow."

The End